help a honey bee

This book belongs to:

_____

Join the Writing Sullivans Readers Club

Visit <u>thewritingsullivans.com</u> to join the Readers Club and receive free printables, updates on new releases, sneak peeks, and monthly opportunities to win signed books and original artwork.

ISBN 978-0-9963020-4-3

ASIN B08L4X4QXH

WET BANDIT

First Edition

Please Note: None of the books in the Animal Sing-Along Series are authored, sponsored, or endorsed by any original artist associated with any song referenced in the Animal Sing-Along Series.

For Rory and Caroline

You're all alone,
working on your flower bed.

You must be thinking 'bout
something that you read…

I'm trying to get
a little pollen
from your flower.

I'm more than happy
to check back here
in an hour.

I know you wouldn't
want me
buzzin'
right by you.

Just like my Queen Bee
who wants all the honey.

I'm prayin' for the day
when I wake up to see
they can make honey in labs,
and I'm finally free...

So if you know a scientist
you think could help me,
tell them to just call or email me,
plea-e-ease.
Help a honey bee-e-e.
Help a honey bee.

Whoops! It looks like
she just might have heard that sound.

She grabbed her hose,
and now she's starting to look around.

Think I'll fly behind this tree
all by myself
and hope she doesn't
see-e-e me.

So much for that,
looks like she's still on my tail.

Why couldn't she just let me be
like she did that snail?

The hose is down.
I'm feeling good about that.

Oh, no! She went
and grabbed a wiffle ball bat.

Whoosh! That was close.
I'm glad that she missed me.

One good shot
and I'll be history.

I'm prayin' for the day
when I wake up to see
they can make honey in labs,
and I'm finally free…

So if you know a scientist
you think could help me,
tell them to just call or email me,
plea-e-ease.
Help a honey bee-e-e.

I'd rather be at home with my family,
or on the beach and
sippin' some sweet tea-e-e-e.
Help a honey bee-e-e.
Help a honey bee.

Oh, you know that I don't
want to have to sting,
but I might not have a choice.
I'd rather plead my case.
If she could only hear my voice.

But all she hears is *buzz*
and the sound made from her swing.
That last time was way too close.
Now I guess I gotta...

But if you know a scientist
you think could help me,
tell them to just call or email me,
plea-e-ease.
Help a honey bee-e-e.

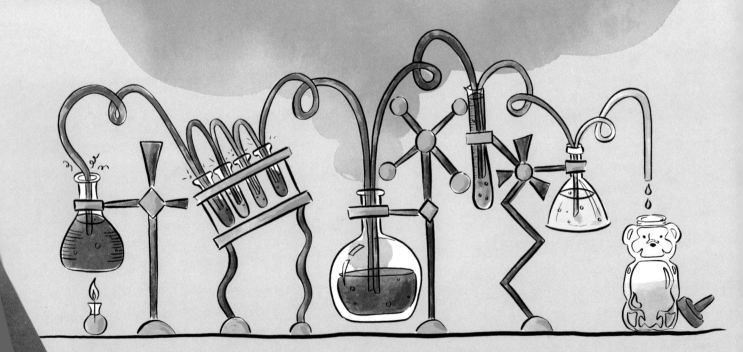

I'd rather be at home with my family,
or on the beach and
sippin' some sweet tea-e-e-e.
Help a honey bee-e-e.

Help a honey bee-e!
It was either her head or me-e-e.
Help a honey bee-e-e.

Help a honey bee.

Made in the USA
Monee, IL
11 October 2022